Park Rangers

Julie Murray

Abdo Kids Junior
is an Imprint of Abdo Kids
abdopublishing.com

Abdo
Kids

MY COMMUNITY: JOBS

abdopublishing.com

Published by Abdo Kids, a division of ABDO, P.O. Box 398166, Minneapolis, Minnesota 55439. Copyright © 2019 by Abdo Consulting Group, Inc. International copyrights reserved in all countries. No part of this book may be reproduced in any form without written permission from the publisher. Abdo Kids Junior™ is a trademark and logo of Abdo Kids.

Printed in the United States of America, North Mankato, Minnesota.

052018

092018

Photo Credits: Alamy, iStock, Media Bakery, Shutterstock

Production Contributors: Teddy Borth, Jennie Forsberg, Grace Hansen

Design Contributors: Christina Doffing, Candice Keimig, Dorothy Toth

Library of Congress Control Number: 2017960554

Publisher's Cataloging-in-Publication Data

Names: Murray, Julie, author.

Title: Park rangers / by Julie Murray.

Description: Minneapolis, Minnesota : Abdo Kids, 2019. | Series: My community: Jobs | Includes glossary, index and online resources (page 24).

Identifiers: ISBN 9781532107894 (lib.bdg.) | ISBN 9781532108877 (ebook) | ISBN 9781532109362 (Read-to-me ebook)

Subjects: LCSH: Park rangers--Juvenile literature. | Occupations--Careers--Jobs--Juvenile literature. | Community life--Juvenile literature.

Classification: DDC 363.6809--dc23

Table of Contents

Park Rangers. 4

A Park Ranger's
Tools. 22

Glossary. 23

Index 24

Abdo Kids Code. 24

Park Rangers

Mae is a park ranger. She loves nature.

Park rangers take care of state parks. They care for **national parks** too.

They make sure visitors are safe.

They keep the park clean.

Joy picks up trash.

They **protect** the animals.

Al helps the elk cross the road.

They do search and rescue.

They watch for fires. The fire danger is high today.

They give tours. Todd talks about the park.

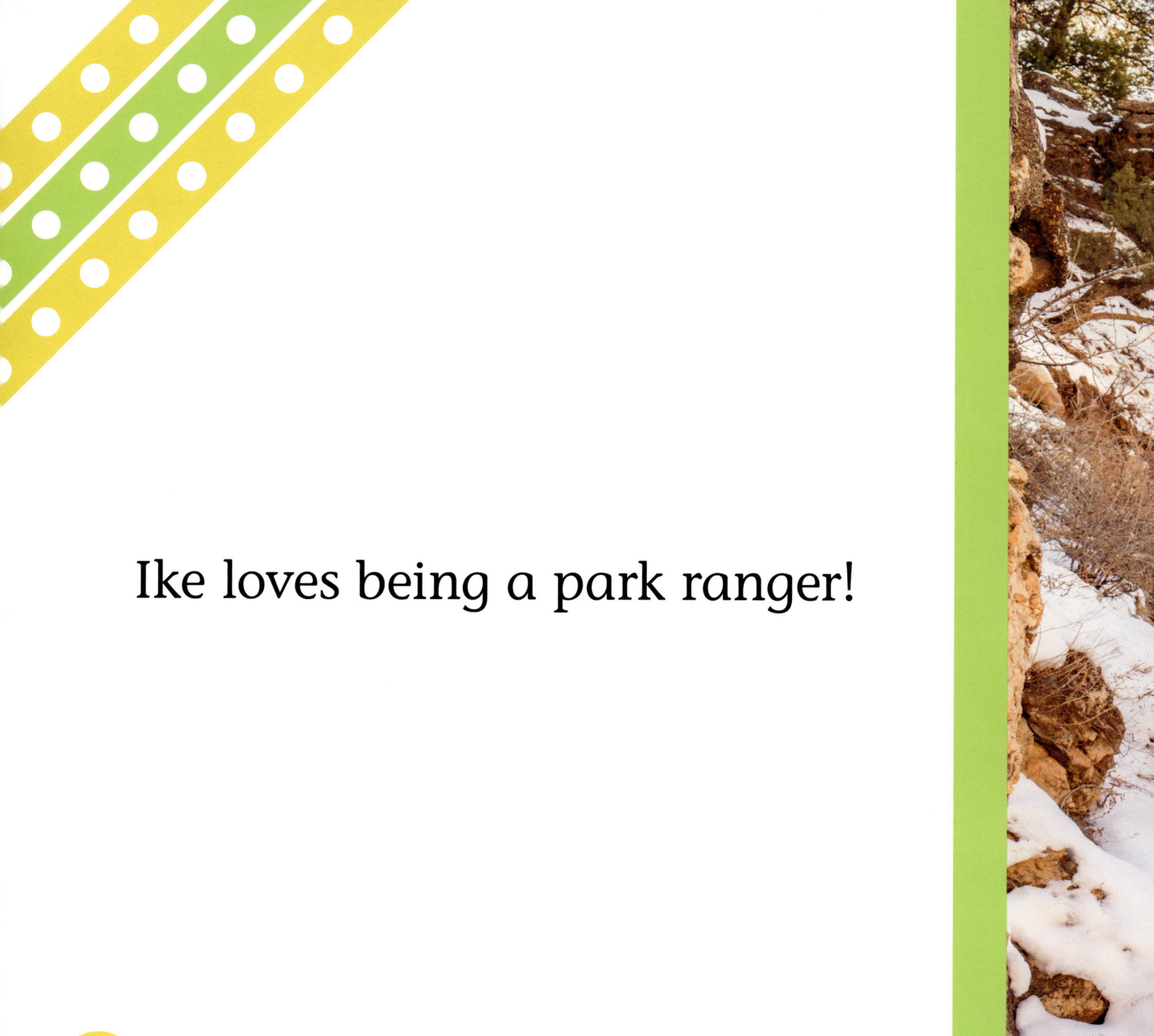

Ike loves being a park ranger!

A Park Ranger's Tools

first aid kit

good shoes

map

vehicle

Glossary

national park
a large area maintained and protected by a nation's government.

protect
to watch over and keep safe.

Index

animals 8, 12

clean 10

fire 16

national park 6

responsibilities 6, 8, 10, 14, 16, 18

search and rescue 14

state park 6

tour 18

Visit **abdokids.com** and use this code to access crafts, games, videos, and more!

Abdo Kids Code:
MPK7894